THE LITTLE RED ROBIN

BY NADIA TOWNSEND
ILLUSTRATED BY SYLVIA FARROW

Nadia Townsend/River Wey Publishing www.nadiatownsend.uk

River Wey Publishing, Osterbrogade 226, St 1, Suite 9, 2100 Copenhagen, Denmark.

Publisher's Note: This is a work of fiction. Names, characters, places, and incidents are a product of the author's imagination. Locales and public names are sometimes used for atmospheric purposes. Any resemblance to actual people, living or dead, or to businesses, companies, events, institutions, or locales is completely coincidental.

Book design © 2017, BookDesignTemplates.com

The illustrations are by Sylvia Farrow (www.sylviafarrowwatercolours.com)

Nadia Townsend — First Edition

ISBN 978-87-94095-00-6

The Little Red Allotment Robin

This book belongs to

....

On a bright sunny summer morning, in a quiet allotment garden, a little robin red breast sits patiently on an old fork, waiting for his lunch to appear.

It is late in the summer, and the little robin has just left his parents' nest. He is looking for a place to build a home of his own.

In a quiet corner of the allotment, he has found a great plot with a cherry blossom tree, rows of delicious fruit and vegetables and an old painted wooden shed.

The next day, the little robin wakes up bright and early. He flies to his little perch on top of an old watering can by the shed. He loves his new home and sings merrily in the morning sunshine.

He spends the next few weeks keeping the gardeners entertained with his cheerful tunes whilst they enjoy gardening in their allotments. It is a very busy time of year, as lots of their crops of fruit and vegetables are now ripe and ready to harvest and eat.

A few months pass, summer turns into autumn and the leaves begin to fall. Then autumn turns into winter, and the weather changes. The days become shorter, and it is dark much earlier in the day. There is a lot of wind and rain. The allotment is quieter now, and the robin sees less of the gardeners, who are not so busy on their plots.

When spring arrives, the allotment comes alive with flowers and cherry blossoms. The little robin flies to his favourite cherry tree to enjoy the sunshine and hops about the branches of the cherry blossom merrily, full of the joys of spring.

He enjoys the longer days and warmer evenings. There are a lot more gardeners in the allotment, and the little robin keeps them all company as they work.

One day, the little robin finds a female robin in the allotment garden. He wants to be friends with her, so he invites her to join him.

Together they decide to build a nest. The little robin gathers moss and leaves and food for his new friend and the female robin spends the day building a cone shaped nest in an old clay flower pot in a hedge by the shed for them to share. Together the two little robins work hard to make the nest soft and safe. They are very pleased with the nest they have made together and soon settle into their new home in the flower pot.

One night, just after his evening song on the roof of the shed, the little robin sees big, dark storm clouds. The wind is very strong. Thunder crashes, lightning flashes and it begins to rain. The little red robin is very scared. The little robin flies back and sits huddled in the nest in the flower pot with his new friend. He is very worried. Will their little nest be strong enough to survive the storm?

Luckily, the little robin's home in the flower pot survives the storm. The flower pot is very well hidden in the hedge, and the robins built a very strong nest, so it didn't move in the storm. The little robins wake up to find a lovely bright sunny day.

Then one day, soon after the storm, the female robin lays a little egg. In fact, she lays a little egg every morning for five days until there are five little white and brown speckled eggs in the nest.

The female robin keeps the eggs warm for thirteen days whilst the male robin flies around the allotment and local gardens gathering food. The little robin looks after his new friend and finds lots of special treats for her. The little robins' favourite foods are insects, worms and seeds.

15

Thirteen days after they were laid, the eggs hatch, and five baby robins appear. They are called 'nestlings'. The little robins are very happy and very busy every day gathering a lot more food after the nestlings arrive!

At first, the nestlings have no feathers and their eyes are closed. Their eyes open after eight days and rows of feather start to appear. After ten days, the nestlings look soft and fluffy, and each has a completely different character. They are all very special and very much loved.

The two little robins look after the nestlings for another twenty-one days. Soon the nestlings grow brown and gold speckled feathers, which they keep for three months until their adult feathers appear.

This little robin surrounded by pretty flowers is two months old. His juvenile feathers have just started to moult, and new red breast feathers are appearing.

When the young robins are fully grown,
they leave the nest to create their own nests,
close by.

This nestling is now an adult robin, as he has
brilliant red feathers on his breast.

One day, he too will find a robin to build a
nest with.

Interesting Robin Facts

As you can see from this map, the European robin can be found in lots of countries in Europe. Robins live all year round in the areas shown in green. The yellow areas are where robins only live in winter, and the orange area shows where robins only live in the summer.

In Victorian times, the postmen who delivered the post wore red jackets. These postmen were known as 'robins'. As the little birds we now know as robins have red breast feathers, they were given the name 'robin red breasts'. Robin red breasts are celebrated across the world on postage stamps like the stamp on the next page. Real stamps used to send letters and parcels have the value of the stamp written on them, for example, 50p or 50c.

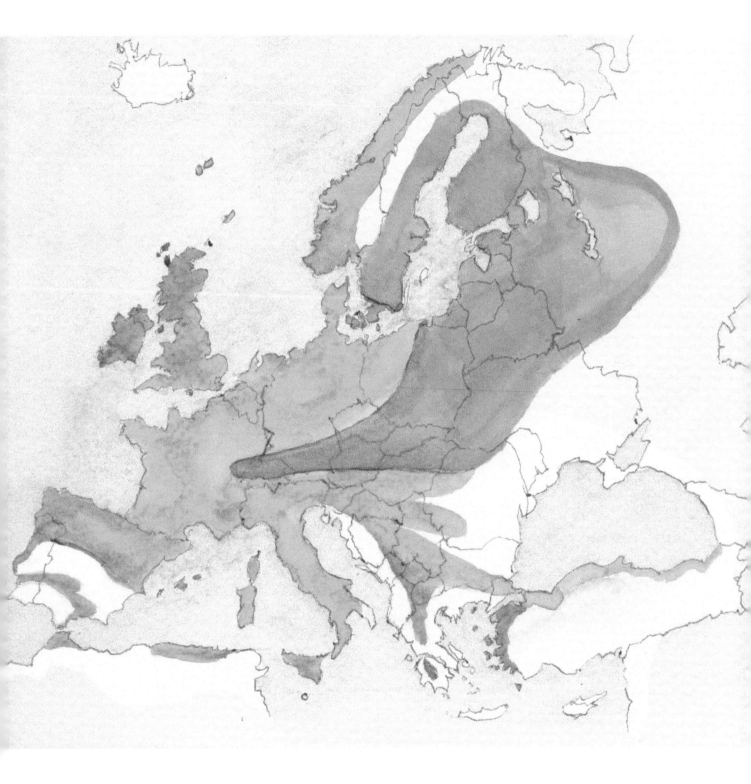

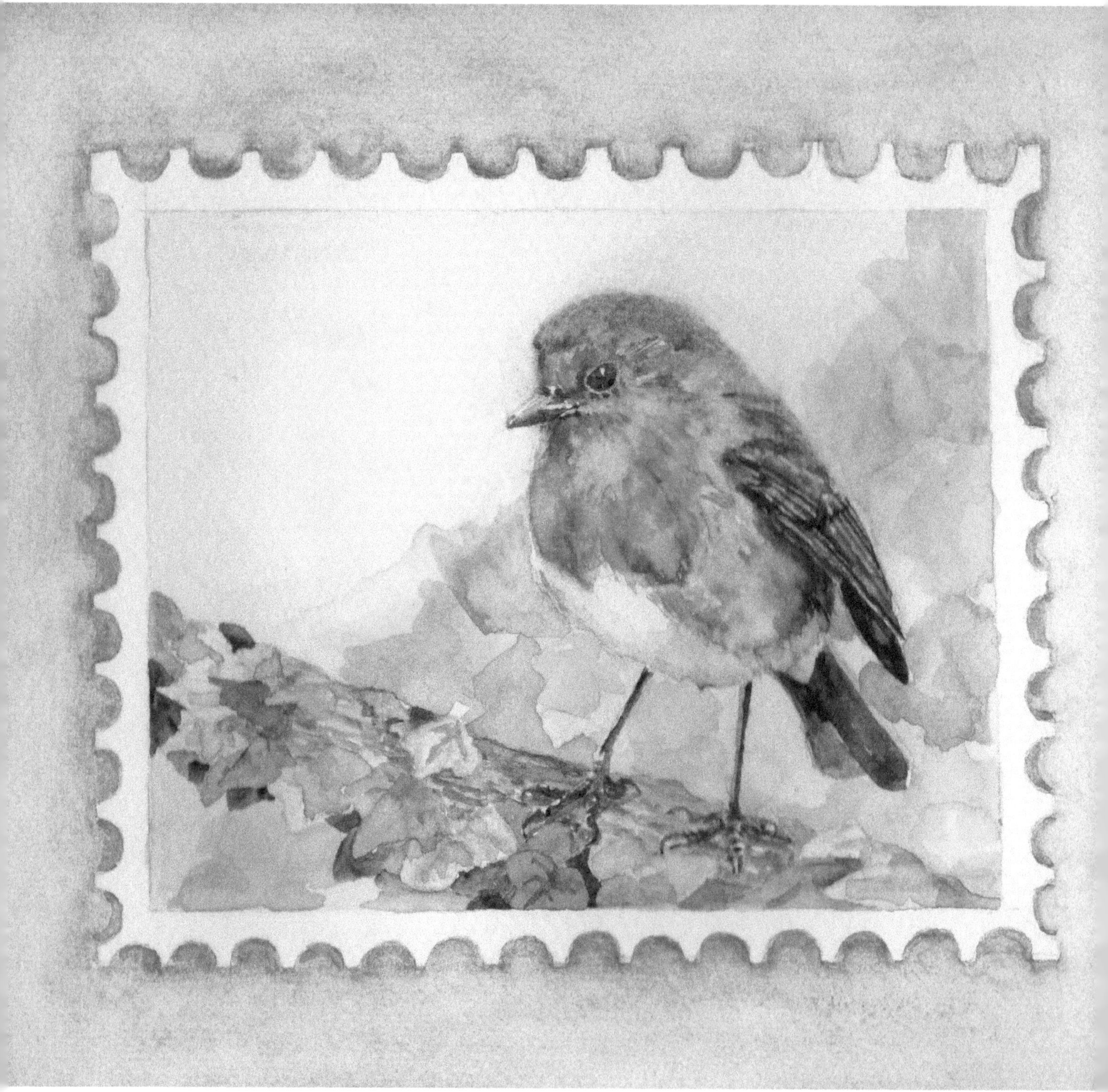

A Robin Quiz

See if you can find the 10 words below:

nest, robin, insect, incubate, eggs, hatch, nestling, moss,
leaves, feathers,

I	N	C	U	B	A	T	E	P	Q
N	B	B	M	K	T	P	V	C	I
S	O	F	E	A	T	H	E	R	S
E	N	M	V	A	D	F	P	L	N
C	R	O	B	I	N	V	I	H	H
T	C	S	V	X	H	Z	E	R	A
N	E	S	T	L	I	N	G	Q	T
E	B	V	S	R	B	M	G	L	C
S	T	L	E	A	V	E	S	P	H
T	A	Q	I	B	V	F	O	U	R

About the author

Nadia Townsend was born in London and is currently living in Denmark with her family. She spent several years working in London as a lawyer before enjoying various other roles and appearing in several films and TV series. She now loves to write stories and non-fiction books for children.

She can be found online at nadiatownsend.uk and www.imdb.com (Nadia Townsend).

Nadia is currently writing a number of other children's books. Updates will be posted on her website soon.

About the illustrator

Sylvia Farrow is an artist and illustrator, who lives in London. She has an art degree from Camberwell School of Art. Working primarily in watercolours, Sylvia has had a series of exhibitions on the theme of birds, a subject very dear to her heart. She has recently completed a commission for illustrations for merchandise from Essex Wildlife Trust and is currently working on various book illustration projects, as well as continuing to develop her own paintings.

Acknowledgements

To my family and friends, whose love and support allowed me to write this book.

Special thanks to Serena Davis.

Thanks also to Sylvia Farrow, whose beautiful illustrations brought my book to life. Sylvia can be found at www.sylviafarrowwatercolours.com.

Thanks to my editor, Marlo Garnsworthy. Marlo can be found at www.IceBirdStudio.com.

Thanks also to my cover and interior designer, Jana Rade. Jana can be found at www.facebook.com/getitdesigned.

This edition is dedicated to Annabel and Benjamin with love xx

Lightning Source UK Ltd.
Milton Keynes UK
UKHW021256201120
373702UK00002B/150

9 788794 095006